A DARK AND NOISY NIGHT

A SILLY THRILLER WITH PEGGY THE PIG

LISA THIESING

DUTTON CHILDREN'S BOOKS ⚡ *NEW YORK*

For Alessandra

DUTTON CHILDREN'S BOOKS
A division of Penguin Young Readers Group

Published by the Penguin Group
Penguin Group (USA) Inc., 375 Hudson Street, New York, New York 10014, U.S.A.
Penguin Group (Canada), 10 Alcorn Avenue, Toronto, Ontario, Canada M4V 3B2
(a division of Pearson Penguin Canada Inc.)
Penguin Books Ltd, 80 Strand, London WC2R 0RL, England
Penguin Ireland, 25 St Stephen's Green, Dublin 2, Ireland
(a division of Penguin Books Ltd)
Penguin Group (Australia), 250 Camberwell Road, Camberwell, Victoria 3124, Australia
(a division of Pearson Australia Group Pty Ltd)
Penguin Books India Pvt Ltd, 11 Community Centre, Panchsheel Park, New Delhi—110 017, India
Penguin Group (NZ), Cnr Airborne and Rosedale Roads, Albany, Auckland 1310, New Zealand
(a division of Pearson New Zealand Ltd)
Penguin Books (South Africa) (Pty) Ltd, 24 Sturdee Avenue, Rosebank, Johannesburg 2196, South Africa
Penguin Books Ltd, Registered Offices: 80 Strand, London WC2R 0RL, England

CIP Data is available.

Published in the United States by Dutton Children's Books,
a division of Penguin Young Readers Group
345 Hudson Street, New York, New York 10014
www.penguin.com/youngreaders
Designed by Jason Henry
Manufactured in China • First Edition
ISBN 0-525-47388-2
1 3 5 7 9 10 8 6 4 2

It was fall.

The trees were down

to their bare bones.

Winds howled.

Leaves crackled.

And Peggy was all alone.

Peggy had not been sleeping well.

Every little noise was giving her the spooks.

"*Oynk,* I'm so tired!" Peggy yawned.

"A short nap would be lovely."

So she lay down for a bit.

Just as she was nearly napping,

sudden... ...ame a tapping!

Tap, tap, tap.

"What was that?"

wondered Peggy aloud.

She heard the noise again.

Tap, tap, tap.

Her eyes were wide open now.

On the window shade,

Peggy saw long, bony fingers.

They went *tap, tap, tap.*

"Oh my!" she said.

"There's a witch

at my window!

What'll I do?"

Quietly, Peggy

snuck out of her room.

She tiptoed down the hall.

She started down the stairs.

But suddenly…

Peggy heard a creepy

creak!

Peggy would take one step—

creak!

and then another—

creak!

She gulped.

"I think a monster is

following me!"

Peggy stood perfectly still.

No *creak!*

"How odd," said Peggy.

She was scared, but

she went into the living room.

She curled up on the sofa.

"I will read for a while.

Maybe I'll relax," she said.

She was beginning to nod off

when suddenly…

she heard

HOOOO! WOOOO! HOOOO!

"Oh no! What was that?"

HOOOO! WOOOO! HOOOO!

Peggy saw something

at the window.

It was white—and

flying up into the air!

"A ghost! It's a ghost!"

Peggy squealed.

Peggy ran into the kitchen.

"I'll be safe here," she said to herself.

Rumble! Rumble! Rumble!

What was that?

She got a little snack,

and the noise stopped.

But suddenly…

Bloop-bloop. Bloop-bloop.

"What now? A slimy,

dripping goblin?"

asked Peggy.

"I need some tea," she said.

Then Peggy heard

a loud screaming!

EEEEEEEEEEEE!

"Aaaaahhh! What's that?

I've got to get out of here!"

said Peggy.

She went into the hall.

Clunkity-clunk! Clunkity-clunk!

"What in the world could *that* be?"

Peggy asked.

Clunkity-clunk! Clunkity-clunk!

Louder and louder.

CLUNKITY-CLUNK!

As Peggy got up,

she bumped the radiator—

hard.

For a moment,

there was silence.

Suddenly, Peggy heard a

rustling sound just outside

her front door.

She gasped. "It could be a mummy!"

Next she heard a rattling sound.

"Or a skeleton!" She gulped.

And then there came

a howling.

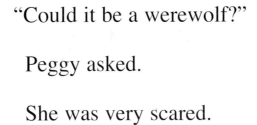

Aaah-whooooooo!

"Could it be a werewolf?"

Peggy asked.

She was very scared.

Peggy thought of all the
noises that she had heard.

Aaah-whooooooo! BLOOP!

CLUNKITY-CLUNK!

EEEEEEEEEEEEE!

Rattly-rattle!

Then she heard

the strangest noise of all.

Tee - hee- hee!

Followed by...

DING **DONG!**

Something was here!

But what was it?

Peggy was very, very scared.

But she went to the door.

Slowly, she opened it just a crack.

Carefully, Peggy peeked out.

She could not believe what she saw!

"Oh, for goodness' sake!" said Peggy.

"Happy Halloween, everyone!"

She gave the mummy,

the skeleton, and the werewolf

some candy.

Then Peggy turned and
went back up the stairs.
She was very tired.

Tap!
Tap!
Tap!

Not even the

tap, tap, tap

of a witch on her window

could keep her awake.